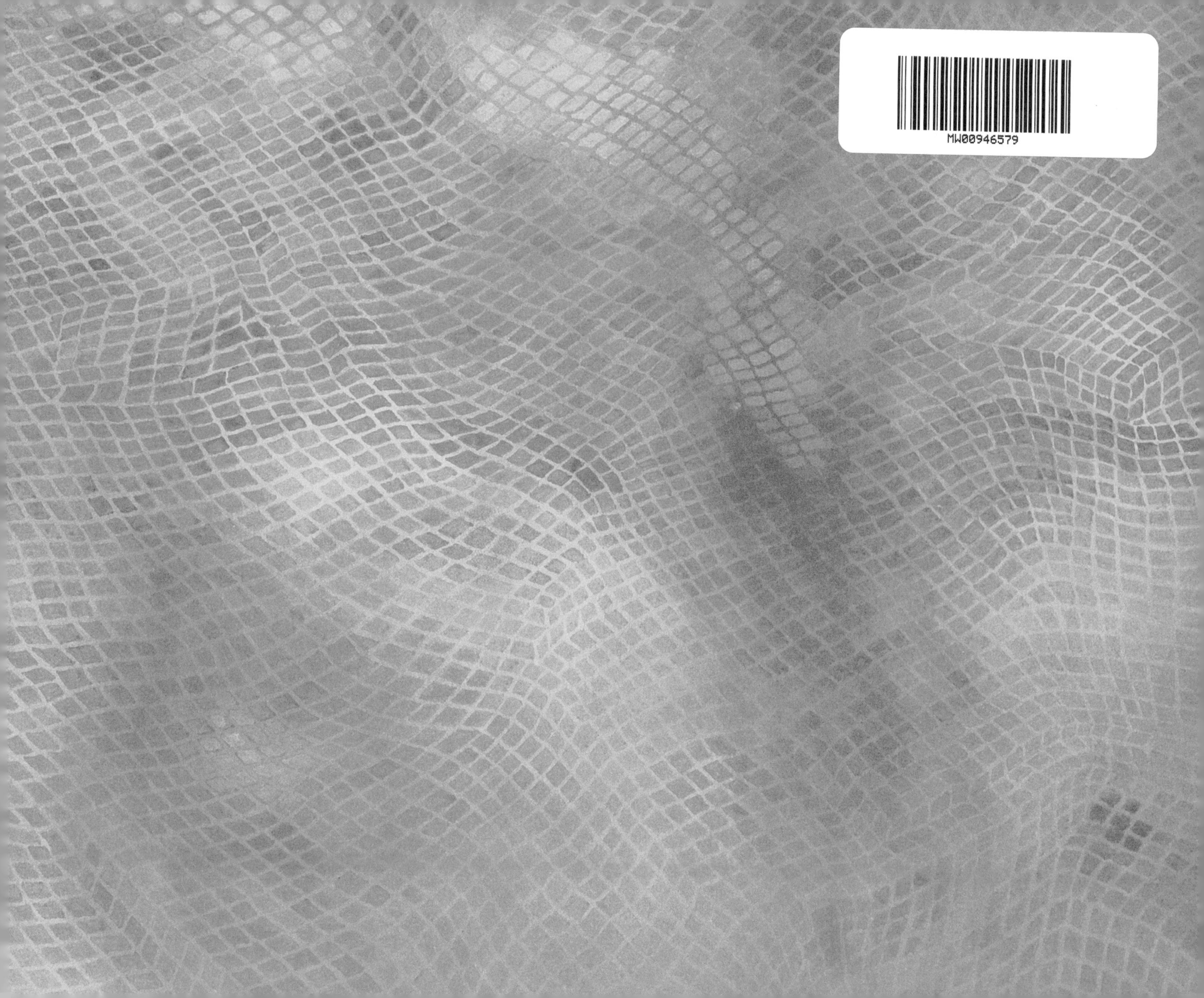
MW00946579

The Goat-Faced Girl

A CLASSIC ITALIAN FOLKTALE

Retold by Leah Marinsky Sharpe

Illustrated by Jane Marinsky

David R. Godine  *Publisher · Boston*

First published in 2009 by
DAVID R. GODINE · *Publisher*
Post Office Box 450
Jaffrey, New Hampshire 03452
www.godine.com

Design & composition by Carl W. Scarbrough

LIBRARY OF CONGRESS CATALOGING-IN-PUBLICATION DATA

Sharpe, Leah.
The goat-faced girl / adapted by Leah Sharpe & Jane Marinsky ;
illustrated by Jane Marinsky.
p. cm.
Summary: When Isabella, a beautiful but lazy young woman, agrees to marry an equally lazy prince, the sorceress who raised her gives her the head of a goat in hopes that she will learn to do things for herself.
ISBN 978-1-56792-393-3
[1. Fairy tales. 2. Laziness—Fiction. 3. Beauty, Personal—Fiction. 4. Princes—Fiction.
5. Magic—Fiction. 6. Foundlings—Fiction.] I. Marinsky, Jane. II. Title.
PZ8.S3402Go 2009
[E]—dc22
2009022383

SECOND PRINTING
Printed at Toppan Leefung Printing Ltd. in China

This book is dedicated to

Ruth S. Marinsky

Once upon a time, long ago and far away, a baby was left in the forest. This event wasn't so strange in itself, for lost children appeared in this particular forest every third Thursday. But this foundling was an infant girl who was far too young for quests, unable to understand talking animals, and even too young to interest the witch in the gingerbread house. Since no one had any idea what to do with her, everyone thought it best to leave her alone.

Three days later a rather large lizard came along. After careful consideration, it picked up the baby in its teeth and carried her home. The other forest dwellers were astonished, but since the baby had become a tripping hazard, they decided not to interfere with the lizard's plans.

As soon as the lizard had returned to its dwelling, it placed the baby on the floor and transformed itself into a beautiful woman. The lizard was really a powerful sorceress, who had heard murmurings about the abandoned child and decided to take the poor baby under her protection and raise her as her own.

Over the years the baby, Isabella, grew into a lovely girl. She was polite, intelligent, and almost everything that a mother would want a daughter to be. Unfortunately, Isabella was also unbelievably LAZY. Some days she stayed in her pajamas until noon because getting dressed was too tiring. She would never walk with her friends to the village pastry shop because it was too far away. She would rather stay in and brush her hair before a mirror than play hopscotch in the forest. And she would never help the lizard-lady gather herbs for her magic. The lizard-lady realized this was not exactly a good quality in a child; but she could not think of a way to change Isabella. Even when she offered to teach Isabella to become a sorceress, Isabella would bat her eyelashes and respond sweetly, "But dear mother, *you* will always be here if I need magical help, won't you?"

So Isabella grew from a lovely, lazy girl into a lovely, lazy young woman.

One day there was a knock on the door. Isabella was busy lying on the couch eating grapes and twirling her hair around her fingers. The lizard-lady opened the door to find a prince. “I am Prince Rupert,” he said abruptly. “I need some food and drink.” With that he marched into the house and flopped onto the couch next to Isabella, knocking over her plate of grapes. With the grapes rolling around on the floor, the lizard-lady served them tea and cakes. Rupert and Isabella eyed each other appreciatively, agreeing on how they loved to be served. The lazy twosome decided they had a lot in common, and by the end of the visit they had decided to marry. Prince Rupert then arranged for a carriage to come take his lovely, lazy Isabella to the castle.

The next morning the lizard-lady watched with dismay as Isabella waved gaily from the departing carriage. She thought to herself, “If she marries him, she will never stop being lazy! She will never learn to do anything for herself! I must stop this marriage before it’s too late.” Then, with a sly smile, the lizard-lady made a sweeping gesture toward the carriage. “I think that should do it,” she chuckled.

At the palace Rupert had gathered his entire court to welcome Isabella, but when she emerged from the carriage everyone froze in horror. Somehow, the lovely Isabella had the head of a goat! As they recovered from their shock, they all began to laugh at the ridiculous sight. The same magic that had given Isabella a goat head, however, prevented her from realizing what had happened. Although everyone else saw a goat head, she smiled sweetly at the crowd, believing she was as lovely as ever.

"I can't marry this monster," Rupert thought, and immediately rushed her off to a tiny cottage on the edge of the kingdom.

When they arrived at the cottage, Isabella was confused. "Where is my beautiful palace full of servants to wait on me?" she asked. "Umm, well, there's this . . . rule . . . in the kingdom . . . you have to . . . pass certain *tests!*" gulped Rupert. "That's it, you have to pass a test before you can, er, marry a prince and get into the palace! And the first test is to, umm, grow turnips. But, uh, if you don't want to you can always give up and go away, er, home." And with that, Rupert fled.

Turnips
SEEDS

For a while, a fuming Isabella stomped around the cottage muttering to herself. She was furious at how badly Rupert was treating her, and she thought longingly of her couch and grapes. However, she was greatly tempted by the idea of all those servants at the palace. After a three-hour nap, Isabella summoned up all her energy and sent a letter to her mother, the lizard-lady, asking for help. She then crawled back into bed; she was sure the lizard-lady would come and take care of everything.

So imagine her surprise when, the next morning, she received nothing but a pile of books, a pair of gardening gloves, a rake, a shovel, and a bag of seeds. She threw up her hands and pulled her ears in frustration, but the thought of a lazy life as Prince Rupert's wife kept her going. After another nap, she opened the books and got to work. Three weeks later, she showed Rupert the few scraggly, sad little turnips she had managed to produce. "Now you can take me to the palace," she said. "I need servants to pamper me. I've been eating only peanut butter sandwiches for weeks, and I am *sooo* hungry."

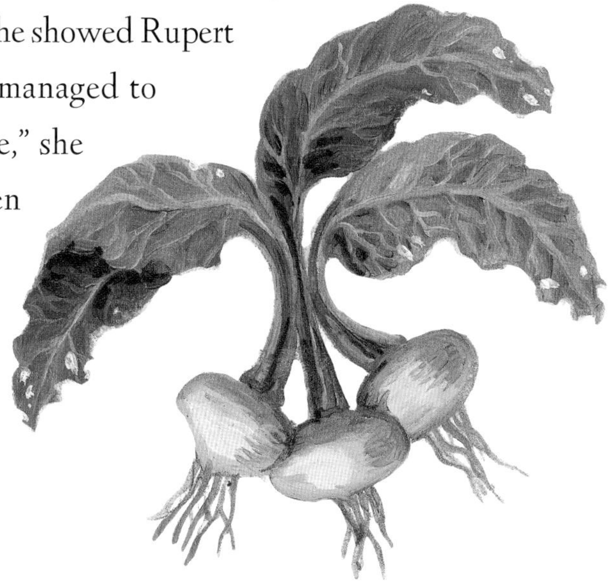

"NO! I mean, no. No. Now you have to . . . you have to . . . prepare a feast worthy of royalty. Or you can give up. I'll send you home in a carriage, a really nice one," blurted Prince Rupert hopefully.

Well, Isabella was so furious that this time she managed to write the note and get it off to her mother without a single nap. The next day Isabella received a package containing cookbooks, pots, pans, and gadgets whose use Isabella couldn't even begin to imagine. When she saw the pictures of appetizers and cakes in the books, her stomach growled. The peanut butter sandwiches suddenly seemed awfully unappetizing. "Well," she said while licking her lips over a picture of roast duck, "maybe learning to cook isn't the worst thing – I mean, until I go to the palace."

After a few mistakes and lots of experimenting, Isabella managed to prepare a tasty-looking meal, not quite a banquet but definitely an improvement over peanut butter sandwiches. Just as Isabella was putting the icing on her chocolate cupcakes, Rupert arrived. With a look of horror he exclaimed, "You did it! Drat! I mean, good. But there's still more. Now you must make your own . . . ball gown! From scratch! But that's *very* hard! Maybe you'd prefer to give up. I mean it has to be *really* nice." With that, Rupert left without another word.

Isabella was puzzled by Rupert's behavior. She furrowed her brow and tried to figure out what was going on. Then she remembered the all-important "Rule of Threes." In any fairy tale or nursery rhyme, it is the third princess, the third night, or the third task that is the important one. She figured this was the standard ordeal all girls in these parts were put through before they could marry princes. After all, in one kingdom nearby, they made the girls sleep on peas. In another, the girls had to attend balls in glass slippers. And as every young woman knows, glass slippers can be pretty uncomfortable.

Isabella decided she would make a fabulous gown.

Without another thought Isabella jumped up and ran all the way back home to ask for help from the lizard-lady. When Isabella reached her mother's house, she wasted no time explaining what she wanted to do. As Isabella chattered away about the design and fabric of the dress, the lizard-lady realized that Rupert's tasks had transformed Isabella into a capable and imaginative young woman.

Three weeks passed. As they worked, the lizard-lady was impressed by how much Isabella had changed. Isabella wasn't merely trying to finish the dress; she was doing extra work to make sure the dress was *just right* – something unique and special. Watching Isabella crouching down to add the final beading to the dress, the lizard-lady decided it was finally time to show her daughter her goat head.

After Isabella stopped screaming, the lizard-lady returned Isabella's own lovely face to her. As the lizard-lady hugged Isabella, she explained, "Darling daughter, I was just afraid that if you remained lazy you would never learn how to do anything." And even Isabella had to admit that she *had* been spectacularly lazy.

Later that day Prince Rupert came by to see the gown. Isabella was very excited. The turnips had turned out all right, the dinner had been pretty good, but the gown was simply perfect. She was *also* wondering how Rupert would react when he saw that her goat head was gone.

Prince Rupert walked in grudgingly, but the moment he saw Isabella his whole manner changed. He swept her into his arms and said, “You’re beautiful again, so now we can be married.” And with that he began to drag her to the palace.

A troubled Isabella asked, "Don't you care about the final task . . . the gown?"

"Oh no," said Prince Rupert. "I just didn't want to have to marry you when you looked like a goat."

By this time Isabella, who really was as intelligent as she was beautiful, was truly furious: "You mean to tell me that you were trying to get rid of me just because I looked funny? You only care about how I *look*? Not who I *am*?" Rupert readily agreed that this was indeed *all* he cared about. Isabella turned to him with her hands on her hips and said, "I am sure I'd be quite bored with someone as lazy and stupid as you." With that, she pushed the stunned prince away from the cottage and told him never to come back.

SPICES
Potions

After the prince departed, Isabella returned to her mother's home. "Mother," she said, "Rupert is a bird brain. I don't want to marry him. He didn't care about me, just my looks. Besides, I'm proud of all the things I can do now . . . and I was thinking, maybe, if you still want to. . . Could you teach me how to become a sorceress?" The lizard-lady was overjoyed. She looked at the lovely, but no longer lazy, Isabella and asked, "What would you like to learn first?"

And that, dear reader, . . .

. . . *is how* this *came to pass* .

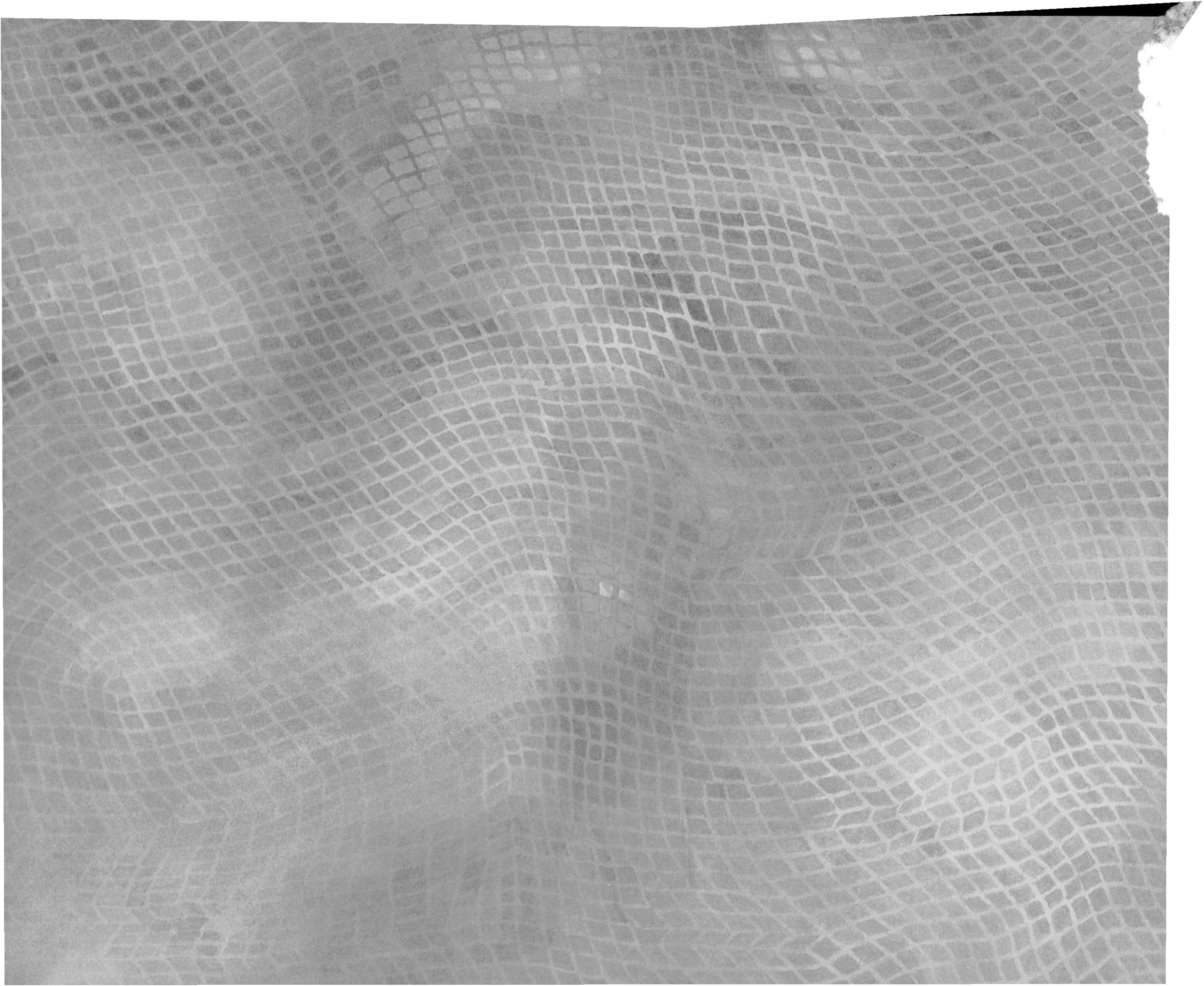